The Quilted Message

D1512276

Ken Munro

GASLIGHT PUBLISHERS

Gaslight Publishers
P.O. Box 258
Bird-In-Hand, PA 17505

ISBN 1-57087-060-8

Production Design by Robin Ober

Professional Press
Chapel Hill, NC 27515-4371

Manufactured in the United States of America
03 04 05 06 07   10 9 8 7 6 5 4 3

This book is for Elisa, Karen, Joyce, and Kim

Special thanks to Joyce,
who said I could and I should.
Also thanks to the East Lampeter Township
Police Department

Table of Contents

Chapter One

The Two-Stepper

"Just wait till you see it," said Sammy, as Brian followed him up the steep steps.

Sammy's bedroom was to the right at the top of the stairway that led up from the shop. The atmosphere of the room reflected that of its occupant. The walls, which had seen many coats of paint over the years, were beige this time with curtains to match. Wall-to-wall bookshelves were filled with encyclopedias, and psychology, how-to, and fiction books. Piles of Newsweek, Time, Readers' Digest, Puzzles and Games magazines were under the bed arranged in a logical and orderly fashion which only Sammy understood. A large map of the moon shared one wall with a window. On the opposite wall an orange and black Orioles' pennant pointed to four award plaques that were presented to Sammy Wilson, 'The Puzzle King', for winning national puzzle contests. Sitting below were boxes and boxes of baseball cards.

Brian, fourteen, short, with wavy brown hair and hazel eyes, always felt important when invited into Sammy's bedroom. It was like being in Batman's cave.

"You must have a million of them," said Brian as he pointed to the baseball cards.

Sammy, a slim boy of fifteen with straight dark hair and serious blue eyes, normally would have delivered a small lecture on the amount of space a million baseball cards would have taken up. But since this was Brian Helm, his very best friend, he announced, "Twenty-seven thousand two hundred and eighteen cards. That's not counting the cards I have downstairs in Mom's shop."

Sammy Wilson's mother started the shop, the Bird-in-Hand Country Store, as a hobby. The shop consisted of four small rooms and a restroom. She sold Amish-made merchandise and antiques. One room in the shop, known as the Quilt Room, had racks of colorful Amish quilts. The business grew and was so profitable that Sammy's father quit his teaching job to help her. And now Sammy was part of it. He started by placing some of his baseball cards on the end of one counter. They sold so well to the locals and tourists that his mother gave him a whole display case for his cards.

"Well, where is it? Where's this super special card you wanted to show me?" asked Brian.

Sammy carefully reached into the desk drawer and produced a baseball card. He cushioned the card in the palm of his hand. "It's a signed Ken Griffy, Jr. Classic Minor League card. I just got it yesterday in a pack of cards I opened."

"All right!" exclaimed Brian as he reached for the

card that showed Griffy in a San Bernardino Spirit base-ball uniform. Ken Griffy Jr. had signed the card himself.

Sammy's blue eyes opened wide as he pulled his hand back. "No, no, no! Nobody touches this card until I put it in a rigid plastic sleeve. I want to keep it in mint condition."

"How much is it worth?" asked Brian, still examining the card from a distance.

"About three hundred dollars." Sammy gently replaced the card back into his desk drawer.

"Are you going to sell it in the shop?"

"I might. I'm thinking about it."

Brian frowned and looked at the computer system that occupied the top of the old, oak desk. He surveyed again the many books, magazines, and baseball cards that helped fill the room. "I wish I was as smart as you."

"Brian, you're always saying that. I was just lucky to get that card."

"I don't mean just that. I mean, like in school, you always have your hand up to answer questions. I bet you get A's on all your tests. And you win contests. You won't find any of those plaques in my room," replied Brian, pointing to the wall. "You always win prizes by selling more candy or subs when we have a fund-raiser."

"You can do the same if you do what I do," Sammy Wilson replied in a reassuring voice.

"What do you do?" asked Brian. His eyes opened

wide. He leaned forward as if expecting to hear the secrets of the universe.

"I read a lot, and I think about things," said Sammy, walking over and picking up a school book. "When school's over each year, I ask the teacher if I can have some of the textbooks we will be using the next year. I read them over the summer in my spare time."

"We all have spare time in the summer," added Brian Helm.

"When school starts in September, I'm ready. I at least have some ideas about the subjects we will be studying."

"Hey, that's smart. What about the prizes you win at school?" asked Brian.

Sammy looked at Brian and smiled. "When do you start to sell the candy or subs?"

"The same day we get the order forms. The day it starts. Right after I get home from school," stated Brian, projecting a what-else-can-you-do? attitude.

Sammy knew that what he was about to reveal would infringe on his own strategy. But Sammy was honest. "I start a week or two before the contests begin. I get customers lined up so that when I come around later, they buy from me."

Brian looked up and to his right. "That's why when I arrive they say, 'I'm buying from Sammy Wilson.' It's like you're always two steps ahead. Right, Sammy?"

"Yeah, I guess."

"Don't you see, Sammy? We're both walking at the same speed, but you're always ahead. Two steps ahead. So you get there first."

"There, you see? You're starting to think the way I do," said Sammy, walking toward his bedroom door.

"I am? Do you think I'm a two-stepper too?" asked Brian, following Sammy to the door.

"Well, you're at least a one-stepper." Sammy smiled as he led the way down the stairs into the shop.

The stairway that led down from the Wilson's living quarters above into the shop was steep. The open stairway allowed the boys to experience the aroma of potpourri, spices, and scented soaps from the shop itself. As Sammy turned the corner to enter the main room of the shop, he stopped abruptly. He was not prepared for the new arrival hanging on the wall.

Amish Album Quilt

Chapter Two

The Conversation Piece

The quilt caught Sammy's attention immediately because he could not understand it. Sammy did not like to not understand something. The only thing he did understand about the quilt was that his mother had bought it the day before at the firehouse benefit auction.

"It's one-of-a-kind, a conversation piece," said Mrs. Wilson to the group of regular locals in the shop who were witnessing the hanging. Sammy's mother was an attractive woman of thirty-nine with blonde hair and blue eyes. She pulled gently at the bottom of the quilt to make certain it was fastened securely to the wall by the two clamps located at its upper two corners.

Sammy was intrigued by the quilt's strangeness. He was trying to determine the reason for the quilt's existence. It contained appliqued pictures - four rows of five picture patches each, twenty figured quilt patches in all. Several pieces of cloth were used to make each picture, and every piece was hand-stitched.

"I've never seen pictures like that on an Amish quilt," said Mr. Wilson, Sammy's father. He was a husky man with black hair and brown eyes. "They don't appear to have any pattern or theme."

"It's an Amish Album quilt," said Mrs. Wilson. "The pictures are to have a special meaning only to the owner of the quilt."

"But they didn't," said a voice from among the spectators. It was Mary Fisher, a young Amish girl who brought Amish quilts to Mrs. Wilson to sell on consignment. She wore a plain, blue dress. Her hair was parted in the middle, rolled and wrapped to form a bun, with a white prayer cap on top. "That's what is so mysterious about this quilt. The owner, Mrs. King, didn't understand the pictures at all."

"That's strange," said Brian.

"I guess that's why she donated it to the fire company auction. She never did like it," replied Mary Fisher.

"Where did Mrs. King get the quilt?" asked Sammy, who by this time had circled the group and was standing behind the counter next to the large wall hanging.

"Amos King, her husband, had it made by our sewing group and gave it to her as a gift," said Mary. "He made the sketches for the patches himself. We still have the drawings."

"Mary, were you there when Mr. King gave the quilt to his wife?" asked Sammy.

"Yes, I was there," replied Mary.

"How did she react to the gift?"

"At first she pretended she liked it. Later she

asked her husband to explain the figures on the quilt. All that Amos King said was, 'That's for you to figure out.'"

"That's odd," stated Mr. Wilson.

Mary Fisher turned, searching the group. "Steve, you were Amos King's hired boy when I delivered the quilt to the wood shop. Do you know anything about the quilt?"

Steven Zook was a young Amish man with a Dutch style hair cut parted in the middle. Because it was July, he wore black cotton pants with suspenders, a short-sleeve, light green shirt, and a straw hat. His thick, black beard indicated he was married. He had come into the shop earlier to deliver his woodcrafts and had gotten caught up in the crowd. Steve had worked for Amos King as an apprentice. After Amos was killed in a fire that destroyed the wood shop, Steve had the shop rebuilt with the help of his Amish neighbors. He continued the business which supplied the local tourist shops with Amish-made woodcrafts.

"No, I don't know anything about the quilt," said Steve abruptly, shaking his head. "How much you asking for it?"

"It's not for sale," answered Mrs. Wilson. "I'm keeping this one for display only."

Lloyd Smedley, a man in his forties, who had a stand at the local flea market leaned over to Helen Wilson and said in a low voice, "All of us were at the auction yesterday so we know what you paid for it. I'll give you a hundred more than you paid."

Sammy knew Lloyd Smedley well enough to know if he wanted the quilt it was worth a lot more. He would resell it, of course. Smedley and money went together like peanut butter and jelly, and his personality was just as yucky.

Mrs. Wilson was surprised at the offer. "No. The quilt is for this wall only."

Mary, who had a receipt for the new quilts she had delivered to Mrs. Wilson, headed for the door. "If you change your mind about selling the quilt, let me know. Good-bye."

Why, thought Sammy, were these people anxious to buy this quilt?

Brian nudged Sammy and whispered, "If they wanted the quilt, why didn't they bid on it yesterday at the auction?"

"Exactly what I was thinking," said Sammy.

"You were?" Brian's frown turned quickly into a smile.

Sammy could tell Brian liked the idea that they were both thinking on the same level. But then Sammy felt himself floating up and away from his friend. Not because he thought himself superior, but because of what he remembered hearing his mother saying to his father the night before. It was what the auctioneer had said as a joke right after she had bought the quilt. "Maybe you'll find some of Amos King's money in it."

The subject of Amos King's hidden money had spiced the atmosphere around Bird-in-Hand for years.

The rumor seemed to be based on fact. Amos King, a dyed-in-the-wool Amishman, ran a very successful wood-craft shop on his farm. He collected rent from his farmland, and he did not trust banks.

As Sammy had once said, "Put them all together and they spell HIDDEN MONEY."

Could this be the reason they wanted the quilt? wondered Sammy. Could they really think the quilt contained money?

"Are these baseball cards in the case all yours, Sammy?" asked Lloyd Smedley.

"Some of them were my father's, but he gave them to me. I have more but these are the cards I want to sell," said Sammy as he moved in behind the counter. "Are you a collector?" Sammy knew what the answer was going to be even before he finished the question.

"No, I just sell them at the flea market. I wouldn't mind having some of your cards. They fetch good money." Lloyd Smedley turned and worked his way through some tourists and headed toward the door.

Sammy studied the two tourists, father and son he figured, who were leaning closer to the glass case inspecting the Nolan Ryan rookie card. Mrs. Wilson followed some tourists into the quilt room to answer their usual questions: "What sizes are the quilts? Are all the quilts really made by the Amish? How long does it take them to make one quilt?" Mr. Wilson stood at the cash register and pulled a charge card through the slot to get an approval number. The female tourist made a final inspection of the hex sign earrings she had just bought. Her husband signed the charge slip while clutching a milk churn.

Steve Zook had Mrs. Wilson's order for more woodcraft pieces and was about to leave when Mr. Wilson mentioned to the tourists that Steve was the Amishman who had made the milk churn they had purchased. As the tourists and Steve walked past Brian and left the shop, they were asking the Amishman how he could work with wood without using electricity.

Brian had been Sammy's friend since kindergarten and knew he was always welcome to visit Sammy upstairs. Upstairs was for socializing. Downstairs was for tourists, customers, business.

"See you, Sammy," interrupted Brian. "You should sell that Ken Griffy Jr. card. My birthday is next week. You could buy me a big gift."

Sammy looked up, shook his head, smiled and waved good-bye.

For the rest of the day, between customers, Sammy's attention was drawn to the mysterious quilt on the wall. He studied the cloth pictures, trying to guess the meaning each picture had for Mrs. Mildred King. The canning jar he could understand. And maybe she had an owl collection. But sixty-one? She was older. The eye? Did she have an eye operation? If Mary Fisher was right when she said even Mrs. King did not understand the pictures, what did it all mean? "That's for you to figure out," came the words Amos King had said to his wife when she had asked the same question.

At closing time Sammy remembered his treasure, the signed Griffy card, that laid unprotected in his desk. He raced upstairs to his bedroom, opened the desk drawer, and carefully picked up the exposed baseball card like it was a fragile butterfly. He pinched open one of the rigid, plastic sleeves he had brought from under the counter downstairs. He gently slid the card inside. Right now, to Sammy this card meant money.

"Dad," Sammy yelled, "I've decided to sell my Ken Griffy Jr. card."

"If that's what you want to do," said Mr. Wilson, walking in through the open bedroom door. "What are you going to ask for it?"

"I thought I'd price it at three hundred. I won't sell it for less. If I can't get three hundred, I'll keep it."

"You might get three hundred from a collector, or tourists from New Jersey or New York," replied Mr. Wilson as he returned to watch the news on television.

"I'm going down now to put it in the center of the case so it will be the first card the customers see. I know where the price stickers are."

Sammy was already half asleep when he went to bed that night. As he closed his eyes and relaxed, he thought of ways to invest three hundred dollars. He pictured himself buying a new ink jet printer for his computer. He might buy baseball cards. Money for his college education would be great. The money could go into the bank. No, he didn't trust the banks. He put the money into the quilt. HOW did he put the money into the quilt? He hid folded thousand dollar bills in the seams. No, he put them behind the twenty picture squares. No, he ground the bills into mush and poured the mush over the quilt, and the mushy money ran quickly from the quilt through the crazy cracks in the floor and, clink, clink, swish...

Sammy opened his eyes. His head turned to the right. The clock displayed 3:20. The noise again. Swish, clink, thud. Downstairs.

Chapter Three

The Break-in

The noise was not loud; it was just out of the ordinary for that time of night. Sammy turned his head to orient himself to the unexpected sound. He raised himself slowly and quietly on one elbow expecting to hear the sound again. He heard nothing. Perhaps a passing car was unusually loud. The metal wheels on the Amish buggies produced a continuous sound along with the clippity clop of the horses' feet. But the traffic noise never bothered him before.

Perspiration drifted down his face as he slowly and nervously slid out of bed. His damp pajamas added evidence to the humidity and mystery in the hot night air. Even the floorboards moaned as Sammy crept quietly in his bare feet to the front screened window. He brushed his straight black hair away from his eyes. If only he could see something that accounted for the noise he thought he heard. Something innocent. Something non-threatning. The bluish glow of a nearby street light spread an eerie effect over the scene below. A police cruiser was parked half a block down the deserted street. Maybe the police were after someone.

He moved away from the window. The feeling was a familiar one. Something he had to do, check downstairs in the shop. They had never experienced a break-in before, but Sammy wanted to be sure. He did not want to disturb his parents. They might think him silly if the reported noise proved nothing more than his imagination.

His bedroom door was left ajar as he moved cautiously down the stairs. Blue light filtered in through the shop windows. He saw no one. As he turned the corner to the main room, he glanced quickly from one side to the other. Again no one. Finally his eyes focused on the wall. All he could see was the wall! The quilt was gone!

The blow came from behind and pushed Sammy hard against the side wall. His face and left side of his body crashed among the would-be Amish souvenirs. As a reflex action, his right arm spun around and got entangled in some cloth. He collapsed to the floor and was immediately covered with bric-a-brac jarred loose from the wall by the impact. A blurred figure leaned over and tugged at him, pulling, pulling. Then nothing.

Sammy tried to untangle his body and his thoughts, but the sharp pain and blurred vision grabbed his mind. He was restricted, helpless. A sliding noise and a thump came from the right. He pivoted his head. Through a bluish haze, Sammy saw the ominous intruder disappearing through the open window.

"What happened? Are you all right?" cried his

dad from the top of the stairs.

"Oh, my gosh! What happened?" echoed his mom as she followed her husband down the stairway.

"Helen, his face is bruised, but there's no blood. He'll live," assured Mr. Wilson.

"I'll get some ice," replied his wife, hurrying nervously up the stairs toward the kitchen.

"Did you fall down the steps?" asked his father.

"No, someone was here. I was hit and pushed against the wall. The picture quilt is gone," announced Sammy with his hands to his head feeling the lumps and the pain.

"No, it isn't. The quilt's here on the floor beside you," said his father as he stooped over and picked it up.

"What?" Sammy could not believe it. "Earlier the quilt was not on the wall and was not on that floor. The intruder must have put it there."

"Here," said his mother who had returned from upstairs, "put this towel with ice on your head. It will keep the swelling down." She handed the towel to her son and noticed the quilt. "Oh, my God! It's torn!" She grabbed one end of the quilt and inspected it. "The whole back is torn apart!"

"The front looks all right. It wasn't touched," said Sammy as he gingerly applied the ice pack to his head. "Why would anyone tear the back of a quilt?"

"That is odd," said his mom. As an afterthought she hurried to the quilt room expecting the worse. She returned greatly relieved. "Thank goodness, those quilts weren't touched."

For the next ten minutes, they canvassed the rest of the shop for damaged or missing merchandise. They found none.

"I guess our visitor was only interested in the quilt," said Sammy as he took the cold, wet towel from his head and handed it to his mother. "Oh, by the way, we may not have to call the police. I saw a police cruiser parked down the street earlier."

As Sammy, still in his pajamas and bare feet, approached the police car, Officer Bill Keener rounded the corner of a house and walked toward him. Bill Keener had been the quarterback on the high school football team and was well-known in the Bird-in-Hand area. He was young with blond hair and blue eyes and was new to the police force. The uniform enhanced his good looks.

Officer Keener acted strange and surprised to see Sammy. "Sammy, anything wrong?"

"Somebody broke into our shop. Did you see anyone running away?"

"Ah...yes, I pursued someone behind the houses and into a cornfield, but I lost him."

"Him? Was it a man?" asked Sammy.

"Oh, I couldn't tell. It was too dark."

When they returned to the shop, Officer Keener recorded the pertinent information: Bird-in-Hand Country Store; owner, Helen Wilson; break-in occurred approximately three o'clock a.m.; suspect came in through side window; took quilt from wall; tore back of quilt; Samuel Wilson, son, age fifteen, heard noise and investigated shop; hit on head from behind with unknown object; quilt left on floor; suspect escaped through open window; not identified; could be male or female; apparently nothing stolen.

Sammy's interest then shifted to the mysterious intruder's entry into the shop. Since the shop had once been a private home, each of the four rooms contained two regular windows. The locking latch on the "port of entry" window was unlocked. Sammy moved in close to find evidence that it had been forced. It had not.

Sammy looked at his parents. "Did any of you unlock this window for any reason?"

"No. You know we always keep them locked," his mother replied.

"Then how did it get unlocked?" asked Officer Keener.

"It could have been someone who was in the shop yesterday," answered Sammy. "Someone who wanted the quilt badly enough to break in."

"But the quilt isn't worth that much," said Mrs. Wilson. "I mean for someone to break in. And why tear it?"

Sammy thought about that for a while and then recalled bits and pieces of his entry into slumberland several hours ago. "For two reasons," he announced. "One, the quilt was not for sale. He couldn't buy it. Two, he thought Amos King's money was hidden in it."

"Well, I can tell you the quilt contained no money," said Mrs. Wilson.

"How do you know that?" asked Officer Keener.

"I felt the quilt. That's the first thing I did when I got to the car after the auction. You know, after the auctioneer joked about the money being in the quilt. I pinched it all over. I know what money feels like, and I know the feel of quilts. There was no money in it," Mrs. Wilson stated emphatically.

"After the auction, did anyone see you search the quilt?" asked Sammy.

"No, I don't think so."

"So our mysterious visitor didn't know the quilt had been searched," added Sammy.

"Not much else I can do here," said Officer Keener. "I'll file this report. You'll probably hear from one of our detectives in the morning."

As his father walked the officer to the door, Sammy wandered over to the window again which was now shut and locked. Why did the young policeman look scared when he saw him at the patrol car? he wondered. And why didn't he dust the window for fingerprints? His fingers tightened into fists. As his lips pressed together, a small crater formed in his right cheek. Blue pierced the squint of his eyes. Sammy did not like being a victim.

The black book was lying on the floor under the window. Sammy bent over to pick it up and felt the effects of the bruises and a slight headache. "This old Bible yours, Mother?"

Mrs. Wilson glanced at the Bible. "No, I'm not selling any in the shop right now."

Sammy opened it to the first page. It was a German, King James version. He flipped the pages quickly. Maybe something was stuck in the Bible that could give a clue to its owner. Nothing. He flipped the pages again with his left hand, reversing the search toward the front of the book. Stop! He saw something. Near the front. Handwriting. A message. In German. And a signature. Amos King!

Chapter Four

The Bible's Message

"**L**ook! There's writing here. It's in German and it's signed by Amos King!"

"I can't believe this," exclaimed Mr. Wilson. "At the same time the quilt Amos King had made for his wife is ripped, we find a Bible containing a message in German signed by Amos King. This is unbelievable."

"It may not be that strange," said Sammy. "I believe this Bible was dropped by our intruder as he hurried to get away. And somehow this Bible and its message has a connection to the quilt. We'll know that connection when we have someone translate the message."

"I know!" said Mrs. Wilson. "Mary Fisher! I'll get word to Mary. All Amish know German and English. They study it up to the time they finish their schooling in eight grade. Mary lives nearby. I can ask if she can come over in the morning after the shop opens."

Sammy looked at his mother. "Do you remember anyone buying a Bible at the auction?"

"No. No, I don't. But they sold a lot of box lots.

You know, whole boxes at a time. The Bible could have been in one of the boxes."

"I was just curious," said Sammy. "Did you happen to notice if Officer Keener was at the auction?"

"Why, yes, he was. As part of security I believe."

They decided they had had enough excitement for one night. They could still get several hours of needed sleep before the shop opened at ten o'clock in the morning. Sammy hurried to the comfort of his bed and the curative power of sleep, for he was still aching.

Later that morning Brian was hopping from one foot to the other at the baseball counter while talking to Sammy. He knew he should not take up space and Sammy's time in the busy shop, but he was excited and wanted to hear all the details concerning the break-in. He winced and shivered when he saw the bruises and touched the lump on Sammy's head. Even though his best friend was trying to downplay the events of the early morning hours, the sight of Sammy and the torn quilt told Brian otherwise.

"Which window did the intruder use?" asked Brian.

"In the front room, the window next to the driveway," said Sammy, pointing to the room next to the main room. "Why did you want to know?"

"Oh, no reason. Well, I watched a police story on television last night. The story was about a psychic who got impressions at the murder scene, and she was able to describe the murderer. I thought maybe, maybe, you know. I thought I might try it," confessed Brian as he headed toward the next room and the window.

"Good luck," said Sammy as he watched Brian turn the corner.

The Bible was sitting on a shelf behind a closed door of the display case waiting for the expectant arrival of Mary Fisher. Sammy was anxious but kept busy re-arranging his baseball cards and hanging framed sepia toned pictures of baseball players to replace the ones sold. The return of Brian helped to fill the time.

"Well, you were at the window for some time. Did you develop any impressions or feelings?" inquired Sammy.

"Yeah, can I use your bathroom?" asked Brian seriously.

"You know where it is," said Sammy, rolling his blue eyes as Brian disappeared up the stairs. Sammy shook his head and smiled.

The digital watch on Sammy's wrist indicated ten fifteen. Soon a young Amish woman would reveal the meaning of the mysterious message written by Amos King. Sammy was hoping it would give meaning to the disturbance of the night before. He opened the display case door, removed the Bible from the shelf, and placed in on the counter top so he could keep an eye on it.

Brian, returning from upstairs, worked his way around some tourists and glanced at the black book. "You scared the mystery guest so bad that he dropped the Bible. Right, Sammy?"

"Or the Bible might have fallen out of his pocket when he climbed out of the window," added Sammy.

Mr. Wilson was arranging merchandise out on the porch. He had hung 'the quilt of the day', an Amish star pattern, on a rod attached to the underside of the porch roof. A different quilt each day was sure to catch the attention and interest of the passing tourists and locals.

Mrs. Wilson had just re-hung the Album quilt. Though tired and angry, she was resigned to the fact the quilt's back was damaged. She stepped back and looked at the frayed edges. "This will be a real conversation piece now. Sammy and Brian, do the torn edges that stick out from the back of the quilt look too noticeable?"

"You can see them," said Sammy. "But you did say you wanted the quilt to be a **real** conversation piece. The torn edges will add to it. What do you think, Brian?"

"The torn edges make it a masterpiece. Why, I'll be having conversations with myself about the quilt for the next two months." Brian's face exploded with his biggest smile.

"What's all the laughing about?" asked Mr. Wilson as he opened the door. "I could hear it all the way out on the porch."

Sammy pointed to Brian. "He made a joke about the quilt being a conversation piece. And speaking of a conversation piece, I've decided to have my own." He reached into the glass case and pulled out his Ken Griffy card. He held it up, peeled off the price sticker and announced, "It's not for sale."

"That's a good idea," said Brian. "You can frame it and mount it on the wall behind the case. Right, Sammy?"

A gentle voice came from the front door. "I can make a little frame for your card if you want."

The tourists standing nearby looked with interest at the slender, young, bearded Amishman wearing black pants with suspenders, short-sleeved pale blue shirt, and a straw hat. Steve Zook was accustomed to being gawked at by some of the tourists and was not phased by the attention he received as he zigzagged through the people toward Sammy. Steve was not interested in the tourists or photos, but he was interested in business.

"I can make the frame and have it ready to deliver with your order next week," said Steve, producing a tape measure from his pocket.

Sammy was a little suspicious of Steve. He had heard stories concerning arguments that had developed between Steve and Amos King when Steve was his "hired boy," or apprentice. Questions arose pertaining to the death of Amos King in the fire. Why did Amos run back into the burning woodshop? Steve had told the police that for some reason Amos had run back into the flaming woodshop and never came out again. Why was Steve so anxious to buy and rebuild the shop? And where did he get the money to buy it? What was Steve doing here today? He had made his delivery of woodcrafts yesterday.

"Yes, do that, Steve. Make a frame and put in a piece of glass for protection," replied Sammy.

Although Sammy's father had been to the woodshop when Amos King was alive, Sammy had never seen the shop. Now might be the time for such a visit. The frame order would give him a reason to investigate the area that was responsible for the recent chain of events. Sammy looked again at the black book resting on the counter. He handed the Bible to Brian and placed the protected Griffy card on the counter for Steve.

Steve Zook wrote the measurements of the baseball card in his notebook. He then turned his attention to the hanging quilt as three tourists entered the shop. A customer had selected a small quilted wall hanging and several pieces of wooden fruit so Mr. Wilson took his position at the cash register. Mrs. Wilson welcomed the three new arrivals to the Bird-in-Hand Country Store and led them to the Quilt Room.

Sammy returned the Ken Griffy Jr. card to his shirt pocket and was cleaning the glass counter when Lloyd Smedley entered the shop. A colorful flat-top hat and a camera slung over his shoulder made him look like a tourist. But unlike a tourist, no one ever benefited a thing, socially or financially, from an association with Lloyd Smedley.

The tattered quilt drew Smedley's attention immemediately. He frowned, turned his head and made a quick observation of the bruises on Sammy's face. "What happened to the quilt? Looks like it has some rough edges."

"Someone broke into the shop last night," answered Sammy.

Lloyd walked around Steve Zook who was still studying the quilt and approached the two boys. "Anything stolen?"

"No, nothing was taken as far as we know," answered Sammy. "The quilt was the only item that was damaged."

"That's odd isn't it? Do you have any enemies?" Lloyd Smedley was still staring at the quilt as if examining it for clues.

"I can't think of any," answered Sammy.

"You don't rip the whole back off of something just for the fun of it," added Smedley, walking back toward Sammy. "Well, the way some kids are today maybe they do."

"That was not done by kids. It was torn by an adult." Sammy looked Smedley straight in the eye.

Smedley looked down into the baseball card display. "Where's your signed Ken Griffy Jr. card?"

"I have it here in my shirt pocket. I was going to sell it, but I changed my mind."

Smedley bent over and carefully examined the cards in the case. "I'll tell you what. I'll give you one hundred dollars for all the cards in the case."

Yes, I bet you would and sell them for five hundred, thought Sammy.

"No, I don't think so," he said politely.

"If you change your mind let me know. And your Ken Griffy card is not worth the three hundred, but I'll give you one hundred dollars cash for it right now."

"No. But you'll be the first to know if I change my mind," Sammy lied.

"Say, I could use a glass display case like this at the flea market. Do you know where I can get one?"

Before Sammy could answer, a voice came from behind them. "I could make one for you just like it," said Steve Zook, taking his eyes from the quilt and smiling at Smedley.

"I don't want to pay a lot of money. How much would you charge?" asked Smedley.

"Let me make a sketch of the counter, and I will give you an estimate later," said Steve as he produced a pencil and notebook from his pocket.

"Better still," said Smedley. "I'll take some pictures of the counter with my camera, bring the pictures to your shop, and then we can get together on the price." He wasted no time in whipping the camera up into shooting position.

Sammy watched as Smedley took shots from different angles. Normally they did not allow pictures to be taken in the shop, but Sammy did not say anything. Instead his attention went immediately to the front door.

As soon as the man entered, his presence dominated the shop. Sammy noticed first his size, tall and heavy set, then his receding hairline and a thin mustache, and finally the dark eyes that could penetrate all of your guilt.

"Good morning everybody, I'm Detective Ben Phillips. I'm here to see the Wilsons." He said that for the benefit of the customers who then started to breath easier. "I heard you had a problem earlier this morning."

It occurred to Sammy that any criminal interrogated by this man would confess immediately. If anybody was going to help him solve this case it would be Detective Ben Phillips.

"How are you, Sammy?" asked the detective, creating an immediate path through the people to the baseball card counter.

Sammy was about to ask how he knew who he was when Sammy remembered he was the only boy in the room with a bruised face.

"How's that head of yours?" continued Detective Phillips. "I read the report filed by Officer Keener. The report indicated you took a nasty blow to the head, and the force pushed you against the wall."

"I'll survive, I guess," said Sammy as his right hand explored the impact area on his head.

Detective Phillips opened a manila folder and glanced over some papers. "According to this report, you didn't get a good look at the intruder. Is that correct?"

"Yes it is."

"That must be the quilt in question," said the detective as he turned to his left. "Odd quilt. Yes, indeed, odd quilt. Well, I'd like to speak to your parents now if I may."

"My mother is in the Quilt Room, and my father is over there behind the counter at the cash register," said Sammy just as Mary Fisher arrived.

The young Amish girl always looked neat. Today she was dressed in a plain, blue cotton dress finished off with a black apron. A white organdy cap covered most of her light brown hair that was always parted in the middle, rolled and then twisted to form a bun in the back. Sammy guessed she must have rushed over to the shop because the cloth strings were hanging down from her cap. Usually the strings were tied in a small bow under her chin.

As Detective Phillips went over to talk confidentially to Mr. Wilson, Sammy took the Bible from Brian who was standing patiently in the corner. Sammy held the black book high in the air and waved it for Mary to see.

Because Mary Fisher was well-known and liked by the Amish and non-Amish in and around Bird-in-Hand, she was acknowledged by all the locals in the shop. She nodded and smiled as she worked her way back to the two boys and the Bible.

"What does the writing say?" asked Sammy anxiously handing the open Bible to Mary.

A sudden silence permeated the shop. It was evident by this time all eyes in the room were on Mary and the Bible. Sammy would have rather it be otherwise, but it was too late now.

"What does it say?" asked Brian who was ready with a pad and pencil to record the translation.

Mary very quietly read the message to herself. She read it again translating the German into English. "'I am afraid Alzheimer's disease. I write this message to my wife. If I go first you will know money location in quilt. You will know. You always do.'"

Mary read it again slowly so that Brian was sure he had every word written correctly.

"According to my report the money was not in the quilt," stated Detective Phillips. He left Mr. Wilson's side, crossed the room, and positioned himself beside the hanging quilt. Bending over, he lifted the bottom of the quilt away from the wall, revealing part of the torn back. "It was not and is not here." He released the bottom of the quilt and with both hands, felt and pinched each square patch of the quilt's front. "The money is not here."

"Maybe that's the wrong quilt. Mrs. King has other quilts," said Mary as she walked quickly to the front door.

"Wait, I'll give you a ride," said Detective Phillips. He knew the Amish religion prohibited the ownership of cars, but the Amish could ride with a non-Amish neighbor. "We can visit Mrs. King together. I want to ask her what she knows about her husband's Bible, and if she donated it to the auction or gave it to someone."

As tourists continued to browse, ask questions, and make purchases, Lloyd Smedley and Steve Zook left the shop still discussing the cheapest way to reproduce the glass display case.

"Well, what do you think?" asked Brian as the two boys studied the quilt.

"This HAS to be the quilt referred to in Amos King's message. Why would he give his wife a quilt in the first place, especially a quilt containing pictures she didn't understand? Amos wouldn't waste money having a quilt made that served no purpose. There has to be a reason, and that reason was his money."

"Yeah, I was thinking something like that," replied Brian. "But what's our next step? Aren't we at a dead end?"

"There has to be something more. We'll just have to break through the dead end. And, I know what our next step will be."

"What's that?"

"Brainstorming!"

Chapter Five

The Quilt's Puzzle

Later that evening, an hour after closing time, Sammy and Brian met back at the shop. From the two chairs placed behind the counter at the cash register, the boys sat facing the Album quilt displayed on the opposite wall. A single overhead light limited the area of concentration to the boys and the quilt. The smell of spices and the hum and coolness from the central air conditioner added rhythm and flavor to the adventurous evening.

Brian was anxious. "Let's get to it. Let's brainstorm. I'm ready."

"Okay," said Sammy, "we'll start by throwing out ideas to each other. No matter how simple or dumb you think they might be."

"You start, Sammy." Brian wanted to follow Sammy's lead.

"It has to be this quilt," suggested Sammy. "Amos King only had one quilt made for his wife. The quilt pattern is weird, but at least it reflected something of himself he wanted his wife to have."

"But his wife didn't like the quilt," responded Brian.

"An album quilt is supposed to contain pictures that are meaningful to that person or family," mused Sammy.

"Maybe the pictures showed too much of Amos and not enough of his wife," said Brian.

"The purpose of the quilt was not to please his wife. It had to do with his money." Sammy and Brian were on a roll. "All right, let's keep going. Keep the ideas flowing," said Sammy.

"Why didn't he just keep his money in a cookie jar and tell his wife where it was?" asked Brian.

"Mrs. King was a talker. You know what I mean? He probably thought if his wife knew, the word would get out. He was a very shrewd man."

"How about this idea? Put the money in a cookie jar and write in the Bible, 'My money is in the red cookie jar on the top shelf.'" Brian felt proud of this one.

"Someone else might accidentally discover the money in the jar. OKAY, now, he had to hide the money someplace where it wouldn't be easily discovered," continued Sammy, picking up steam. He wanted the brainstorming to stay on course. He pointed to Brian and said, "So...."

"He hid the money in the quilt. No one would expect it to be there," replied Brian.

"No, Amos didn't have his money put into the quilt by the Amish quilters. Not if he wanted it to be a well-kept secret, which we know he did. So he would have to unstitch the seams to insert the money into the quilt. He wouldn't do that. It was too much trouble," concluded Sammy.

Brian walked over and ran his hands over the squares of the quilt. "It really is a puzzle. Right, Sammy?"

"Yes, yes, maybe it is!" shouted Sammy. Quickly he held up the paper that contained the translated message. Both boys re-read the words. They re-read them again. And there it was! "If I go first you will know money location in quilt."

Sammy immediately thought about the optical illusion picture he had seen in a book that showed something like a vase OR two faces depending on how you 'saw' it. This time Sammy 'saw' the other interpretation of the words.

"Of course," proclaimed Sammy, "the quilt contains the information about the location of the money."

"Sure," said Brian. "It's easy when you take the note and, read it again for the first time."

Sammy burst into uncontrollable laughter. It was rare for him to display his emotions. But this was a special occasion. Sammy did not like dead ends, and Brian had just helped to open one and lined it with humor.

"It's the pictures on the front of the quilt," said Sammy shifting logical gears. "The pictures contain the secret to the location of the money."

"It looks complicated," added Brian. "How did Amos King expect his wife to solve it?"

"I just remembered something," stated Sammy.

"When I won my first crossword puzzle contest, Amos King congratulated me. He said his wife also enjoyed doing crossword puzzles and was quite good at it. That's what he meant in his message to his wife, 'You will know, You always do.'"

Sammy grabbed a pencil and a large white paper bag from under the counter. He drew twenty squares, four rows with five squares in each row.

"I need your help, Brian. Let's work together on this."

"You need my ideas. Right, Sammy?"

"Absolutely," answered Sammy. "I noticed that each block contains one object. What do you make of that?"

"I'm not sure," said Brian.

"Maybe each object represents a letter. Remember, Mrs. King was good at crossword puzzles. Which would mean that each block gets a letter," suggested Sammy.

"Yeah, I think you're right."

"Brian, you don't have to agree with me all the time. I'm not always right," said Sammy.

"You're right most of the time. And if I agree with you all the time, I'll be right most of the time. It's better than being wrong most of the time." Brian produced one of his warmest smiles.

Sammy looked away and smiled. Even he found it hard to disagree with this kind of logic. It reinforced what he already knew. He enjoyed Brian's comfortable humor.

"Let's go with the latter idea," said Sammy. "I'll write in each square, a possible letter represented by the object in the square."

Brian started with the first row. "J for jar."

"Could also be a C for canning jar," added Sammy. "Okay, the first square could be letters J or C. The second square must be O for owl. Third square."

"A for age," said Brian, "if sixty-one was Mrs. King's age when she received the quilt."

"All right, we'll put an A in square three. Could also be N for number," added Sammy as he also included an N.

"An I for square four," said Brian, picking up speed.

"An E for the word eye," added Sammy. "And a Y for yoke." He placed a Y in the last square in row one. "Now, can we make a word?"

"JOAIY, CONEY, JONEY," offered Brian. "If we could get an H for the first picture, we would have HONEY."

"If the first square had an M, the word could be

money, which sounds logical."

"How can we get an M for jar?" asked Brian.

"What's another word for canning jar?" Sammy asked knowing the answer.

Brian thought of the canning jars his mother had at home. "A Mason jar. M for Mason."

Sammy nodded in agreement. "Right, so we'll print MONEY for the first word of our puzzle."

"This is easy. Right, Sammy? Next row, H for heart."

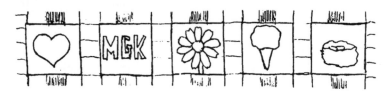

"Or L for love." Sammy placed an H and an L in the first square in row two.

"Next might be Mrs. King's initials. I know her first name is Mildred. Does that sound right?" asked Brian. "I wonder what the G stands for? Maybe, Gertrude." Brian smiled.

"Sounds good to me. How about L for letters?" Sammy printed out an I and an L.

"F for flower," said Brian.

"D for daisy," replied Sammy. "Any more?"

"Can't think of any."

"Square four. I for ice cream. Might be C for cone."

"Square five. N for nest." Brian waited for Sammy to catch up in printing the letters.

"What does that give us for row two? HID IN," said Sammy, answering his own question. "Money Hid in."

"The next two rows will tell us where it's hid." stated Brian. "B for Bird. M for mail."

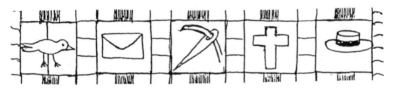

"Hold on! Slow down! We don't want to get sloppy now. Take your time. First square, row three, B for bird. Could it be something else?" asked Sammy.

"A line or a stick is going through the bird. Maybe it's a dead bird." Brian grinned.

"Let's go with B for bird. Next you said M for mail. Okay, but it could be E for envelope." Sammy noted the letters in the appropriate square.

"N for needle," said Brian.

"C for cross and H for hat. That gives us BENCH, bench," replied Sammy allowing his subconscious to assist. "Money hid in bench."

"One more row to go!" exclaimed Brian.

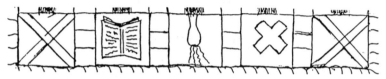

"First square, row five. It looks like it's crossed out. Same for the last square in the row."

"We don't count those. Right, Sammy?"

"Square two. Book. B for Book. O for onion and X for **box**! Sammy pointed to the puzzle quilt and added, "Got you! Money hid in bench box!"

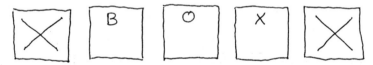

"There's no puzzle that we can't solve. Right, Sammy?" Brian slid into deep thought. "What's a bench box?"

"That's a good question. It might be a bench that has a hinged seat. You lift the seat and you have storage space underneath, like a... deacon bench. Yeah, Amos King's money must be hidden in their deacon bench!"

Chapter Six

The Dead End

Eight o'clock the next morning, the boys pedaled their bikes along the edge of the road that led east from the Bird-in-Hand Country Store. They had decided that because no way existed for them to communicate with Mrs. King the night before, they would visit her with the good news in the morning.

Sammy and Brian had to contend with the locals driving to work, the tourists' cars and RVs, and the Amish buggies. The Amish buggies set the pace. Time almost stood still as the boys watched the tourist traffic piling up behind the slow-moving buggies. When room allowed, the buggies hugged the rim of the road permitting the impatient modern world to pass them by.

The boys turned off onto the next narrow road, their bikes heading in the direction of the King farm. Before them lay the gentle rolling hills of Amish farmland with no telephone poles and electric wires to clutter the scenery and their lives. They rode past fields of fresh corn waiting for the next rainfall. A young Amish teenager was riding a scooter reflecting a simple mode of transportation.

"Should I challenge him to a race, my bike against his scooter?" joked Brian.

"You better not," said Sammy. "He might win."

Up ahead a small, simple sign announced Steven Zook's woodcraft shop. Mrs. King's farmhouse was located at the end of a long lane that ran beside the shop. Sammy glanced at the rebuilt woodshop as he turned right into the lane. He would stop later to visit. Right now he was anxious to bring an end to the Amish quilt mystery. Brian followed behind as the two bikes traveled the long lane to the farmhouse.

The boys propped their bikes against a tree and walked around to the kitchen door. Since the kitchen was the center of the Amish family activities, its entrance was considered the front door of the house.

The old lady appeared upset and surprised as she welcomed the "English" boys into her kitchen. Since her husband's death in the fire, Mrs. King lived alone and had only Mary Fisher to help with the chores and provide buggy transportation. Mrs. King was barefooted and wore a black cape and apron over a plain lavender dress. A white cap covered most of her gray hair, and the wire-rimmed glasses revealed sad eyes that were yearning for long overdue good fortune.

"Everything is a little much for me right now. I have it so in my back you know. First, Mary and a detective came yesterday and asked questions about the quilt and Amos' Bible. They said Amos' money was in one of my quilts already. We looked at the only two I have." Mrs. King shook her head. "No money."

"We know," said Sammy. "That's why we're here."

"And then," Mrs. King continued, "someone came in the house last night. The kitchen window was open."

Sammy did not want to hear this. Another opened window. Another intruder. Was it the same person who had entered the shop? He concluded the intruder was again one step ahead of him.

"Was anything taken?" Sammy was hoping she wouldn't say the deacon bench.

"Nothing was taken, but such a mess!" She motioned and moved aside to afford them a better view of the kitchen.

The walls were painted lettuce green, reflecting one of nature's colors. Near one corner was a wood stove, a needed source of heat for the winter. Bottled gas was used for cooking and for heating the well water. The windows contained no curtains but had dark green shades. Potted plants that once lined the opened window were neatly placed on the floor beside the window, showing the concern and experience of the intruder.

Sammy noticed the wooden benches that normally had surrounded the kitchen table were either upside down or lying on their sides. In another corner was a deacon bench with its lid up and clothes thrown about on the shiny linoleum covered floor.

"Wow! This looks like my bedroom," said Brian as he hurried over to the bench. His tennis shoes squealed on the linoleum. As he surveyed the mess, he said, "Somebody got the money! The bench is empty!"

Sammy's shoulders dropped as did his hope of finding the money. "Mrs. King, do you have any other deacon benches?" inquired Sammy. "Any in the woodshop?"

"No, that's it. I keep old material in it that I use to braid oval rugs. I use it all the time. Amos' money was not in the bench if that's what you mean."

"No, you're right," Sammy reassured her. "Amos would not have hid his money where it could be discovered so easily." He bent down and inspected the inside of the bench looking for a false bottom. He found none.

"Well, I'll tell you boys. It wonders me. I searched everywhere already in this house after Amos died. I know Amos ain't, but the money is. I know the money is because Amos wasn't much for banks."

"According to what your husband wrote in his Bible, your quilt that my mother bought at the auction contains information about the money. Did your husband ever hint to you that the quilt had a connection to the money?"

Mrs. King shook her head. "He knew I didn't like the quilt. He would say, 'Some day you'll figure it out.' From what you boys have said, you thought you had it solved."

Sammy and Brian showed Mrs. King the sketches

they had made of the twenty squares. They explained the steps they had gone through to arrive at their solution. Maybe she could find something they overlooked.

Mrs. King agreed that the quilt was like a cross-word puzzle and that each square represented a letter. "In the third row, the first four squares could spell bent."

"But why the H for hat after that?" asked Brian.

"Money hid in bent H box. Money hid in bent hat box," said Sammy. "Does that mean anything to you, Mrs. King?"

Mrs. King thought for a moment. "No, nothing. But if the bird was a thrush and the cross was a T, that becomes tenth box. Which ... means nothing either. The only boxes I know are the large toolboxes Amos had in the woodshop. There are only three and Steve Zook uses them now."

"Before we leave, Mrs. King, can you tell me about what time the break-in occurred last night?"

"I'd say about three o'clock."

Sammy felt greatly disappointed and depressed as he and Brian returned home and ended up in his bedroom. Someone was beating him to the punch. This same person was getting answers faster than he was. He didn't feel like 'King of the Puzzle Hill' anymore. Who was the mysterious three-o'clock-in-the-morning intruder?

Sammy walked over to Brian. He felt defeated. Fortunately, he was not going to give up. "Brian, I think our window intruder is someone we know. Who would you include in our list of suspects?"

"If it was me," stated Brian, "I wouldn't have a list. Only one name. Officer Keener."

Sammy was surprised and pleased that Brian was growing - independently. He wasn't accustomed to Brian being so assertive, so independent in his thinking. Sammy wanted to test if there was substance to Brian's opinion. "Why? Why do you suspect Officer Keener?"

"Who has night duty and drives around Bird-in-Hand at three o'clock in the morning? Whose car did you see parked down the street at the time of your break-in? Who had a strange look on his face when he saw you at his car? Who didn't even bother to test for fingerprints on the window? That's pretty good. Right, Sammy?"

"I just thought of another reason to suspect Officer Keener. I don't know why I didn't think of it before. Officer Keener was not out of breath when he told me he had chased and then lost the intruder in the corn field. He was not breathing hard at all."

"That's enough for me. He's the one," announced Brian.

"We're not going to accuse anyone until we have proof. Our intruder could be any of the regulars in the shop. They were all at the auction. They saw my mother buy the quilt. They heard the remark about Amos' money being in the quilt. Any one of them could have bought the box that contained the Bible. They all wanted to buy the quilt from my mother. But one of them did manage to almost solve the quilt's message."

"This whole mess is turning out to be a more challenging puzzle than I thought," moaned Brian.

"Let's look at the puzzle from a different angle," suggested Sammy as the boys were getting nowhere.

"How's this?" asked Brian, lying down on the floor and looking up at the ceiling.

"That's not what I meant."

Brian frowned, got up slowly from the floor, and darted over to the large map of the moon. He grabbed it from the bottom, pulled it away from the wall, and ducked underneath. The back of the poster resettled over his face.

Sammy couldn't believe what he was seeing. "Brian, what are you doing?"

"I want to see what the other side of the moon looks like." Brian bent down again, stepped out from behind the poster, and looked at Sammy, expecting to see at least a smile.

Sammy stood frozen, his face half holding onto the start of a big smile and half revealing deep inner thought processes. "I had a nagging feeling since yesterday about something and now I know why. Brian, you just told me who our mystery intruder is! Now if we can only solve the quilt puzzle, I can prove it!"

"I know I told you who the intruder is, but I wasn't listening. Who is it?" Brian wondered.

"I don't want to say until I can prove it."

"You're not the National Inquirer. Right, Sammy?"

"The picture I don't quite understand," said Sammy, getting back to the twenty squares, "is the first picture in the row three, the bird. What kind of bird would have something going through it?"

"Beats me," responded Brian. "But let me try something." His lips started to move and his head jerked up and down. His lips and head stopped and he frowned.

"What were you doing?" asked Sammy.

"I was replacing the b sound in the word bench with the sounds of the other letters of the alphabet. The only word that sounded right started with an R for wrench. But wrench starts with WR."

As Sammy thought about what Brian had just said, everything fell into place. "Brian, that's the key to the whole quilt puzzle," exclaimed Sammy. "That line isn't going through the bird. It's going through the square dividing the square in half. Amos King needed a six letter word in line three so he divided the first square into two."

"But what kind of bird starts with a WR?" asked Brian.

"A wren," answered Sammy. "If we're right this time, the money is hidden in the wrench box. Remember Mrs. King saying this morning that her husband had several large toolboxes?"

"Yeah, three, and one of them has to be a wrench box," said Brian. "The Amish don't use electricity because of their religion. All of their tools are pneumatic. They run by compressed air which means pipes and fittings."

"Brian, I have something very important to do. I'll meet you in two hours at Steve Zook's woodshop."

"Where are you going? What are you going to do?" asked Brian.

"You know what we say in Bird-in-Hand. A bird in the hand is worth two in the bush. But since we don't have the bird in our hand, I need to shake the bush. And then I'm going to kill two birds with one stone."

Chapter Seven

The Green Treasure

This was the first time Brian had been to an Amish woodshop. After he propped his bike next to Sammy's at the front right corner of the country-red building, he went inside. Two crude-looking ceiling fans with thin metal blades moved the hot July air. A fifteen-foot fan belt traveled between the two fans transferring the energy from a compressed air motor. Such a long fan belt never existed in Brian's world. Eight-inch diameter pipes rose from each of the seven woodworking machines. They traveled across the unfinished drywall ceiling to the vacuum producing holding tank containing sawdust.

Two young Amish boys were working quietly at a back table. Both dressed alike, workshoes, black cotton pants with suspenders riding over pale green shirts. Long, dark gray aprons protected their clothing. Even inside this building, they wore the straw hats. One boy brushed oak stain over pieces of oak wood that would become part of a child's chair. The other Amish boy wiped off the excess stain and set the wet pieces onto a drying rack.

Many crude S-shaped wires hung from the two-inch pipe that carried compressed air to the various machines. Unlit propane lanterns hung from several of these hooks. Many windows provided the light needed for the work day. When work continued into the darkened evening hours, the propane lanterns would be lit and hung over the work areas. Brian knelt down and petted the beautiful, sand-colored cat that kept the shop free from field mice and rats.

Sammy, Steve, and Mrs. King were busy talking at a large worktable when Brian joined them.

"I've explained to Steve and Mrs. King," said Sammy, "how we think we've solved the quilt's puzzle. If we're right the money should be in this toolbox."

"I don't think there's money in that box," insisted Steve. "I've took wrenches from that box several times to do work on the air hoses. I didn't see no money."

Sammy lifted the lid and took the wrenches out one at a time. He knew that most large toolboxes had a lift-out tray. When it was empty, he pulled up on the tray. It would not come out. He wiped the heavy grease from his hands and tried again. No luck.

"That tray is rusted in," said Steve. "Amos told me even he couldn't get the tray out. We just used the top part."

Sammy picked up the old, greasy paper from the bottom of the tray. "Well, look here! No wonder you couldn't lift the tray out, there's a screw in each of the four corners." A sly look and smile reflected the growing anticipation in Sammy's actions.

"I got a screwdriver right here on the bench," replied Steve.

"Steve, suppose you loosen the screws then Mrs. King can have the honor of taking them out and lifting the tray."

Mrs. King was very nervous as she backed out the last screw. "Oh, I'm so befuddled yet. If you don't mind, I want to say a little prayer before I pick up the tray."

They all bowed their heads.

"Lord, I never asked for much, and I'm not asking for anything now. I want to thank these English boys for what they've been through to understand Amos' puzzle. Lord, Amos thought he was doing right by what he did. He picked a strange way to do it, and it spites me so. But, Lord, you know Amos. Please be with us now and always, Amen."

They all raised their heads, and all eyes were on the toolbox as Mrs. King slowly lifted the tray.

"Heavens be praised!" said an emotional Mrs. King.

The toolbox suddenly turned into a treasure chest. Green treasure. Money. Stacks. Held together with rubber bands.

"It's the pot of gold at the end of the puzzle. Right, Sammy?"

"But it cost Amos King his life," said a somber Sammy, taking the edge off the bit of humor. "Amos ran back into the fire to retrieve his box of money."

Mrs. King was deep in her thoughts. She would have given up the money to have Amos back.

With the money stacked on the worktable still bound with rubber bands, Sammy and Steve agreed after doing some paper work, the total amount came to about two hundred thousand dollars.

Mrs. King reached under the worktable and selected an old, paper grocery bag which she opened and set on the floor. Very carefully she and Steve filled the bag with the money.

"All that money being held together with rubber bands and a used paper grocery bag," said Brian as the two boys watched.

Sammy smiled, raised his eyebrows, and tilted his head. "That's the Amish way. Keep it simple."

Steve Zook replaced the tray and the wrenches and returned the toolbox to the corner. Picking up the bag of money, Steve said, "Come, Mrs. King, I'll walk you back to the house."

"You have a lot of money there. May I ask what your plans are?" asked Sammy.

"So I don't work myself up so hard already, the bag goes to the bank first thing Monday morning." Mrs. King headed for the door.

It appeared to Sammy the deep wrinkles that lined her aging face were somehow dissolving, and that even the Amish understood the power of money.

"Oh, Steve and Mrs. King, remember what we

talked about earlier and rehearsed," said Sammy. "It could happen at anytime. Please be ready. Oh, and don't tell anyone about finding the money."

Outside, Steve placed the two-hundred-thousand-dollar grocery bag into a small, wooden wagon and pulled it behind him as he followed Mrs. King up the long lane to the farmhouse.

"What's that all about?" asked Brian. "It could happen at anytime. Please be ready."

"How would you like to be with us tonight when we catch the intruder?"

"No, I can't tonight, Sammy. I'm watching cartoons on television." Brian grinned. "Of course I want to be with you! You couldn't keep me away! Where? When?"

"Be at my house at one o'clock in the morning. Detective Phillips will pick us up. Oh, and I'll have flashlights for both of us."

"At one o'clock in the morning? You mean like late tonight?" asked Brian in disbelief.

"Yeah, you're going to miss your beddy-bye time. Tell your mother you can sleep over with me. If I have this figured correctly, we should be in bed by five tomorrow morning."

Chapter Eight
The Stakeout

It was one o'clock in the morning when Detective Phillips picked up Sammy and Brian in front of the Bird-in-Hand Country Store. The detective had been filled in earlier that day by Sammy about the possible solving of Amos King's puzzle. Clues that led to a likely suspect were also discussed. Phillips had agreed that enough cause existed to set up a stakeout. Since he had experienced plenty of stakeouts before, he knew sometimes they worked, sometimes not. But he was willing to give Sammy the benefit of the doubt. An element of danger was involved; the suspect could be armed. You could never predict what a person would do when backed into a corner.

Brian sat alone in the back seat of the car. He had one of Sammy's flashlights and was excited at being involved in an adventure with his best friend. Disappointment was present however, because Sammy had not confided in him in regard to the suspect's identity. But he understood Sammy's strict rule about people being innocent until proven guilty. Sammy was not a person to gossip, but only looked for that "predictable pattern."

Could Sammy be in over his head on this one? Brian wondered. This was different: a real stakeout, a real detective, a real police matter, a real criminal. Of course, on the other hand, Sammy did solve a real puzzle, discover real money, develop a real suspect, and could have us in real trouble if this doesn't work out. Brian automatically smiled to himself and glanced at Sammy sitting in the front seat. It helped.

Space and darkness increased as the car left the lights of Main Street and entered the narrow country road. Sammy was remembering the last picture he had of Mrs. King, heading up the lane with a bag of money trailing behind. He realized the success of catching the suspect in the arranged surveillance depended on word not getting out regarding the discovery of Amos King's money. In a small community like Bird-in-Hand, word spread quickly. Success relied on secrecy. As they continued on the back road, Sammy decided not even to mention the discovery of the money to Detective Phillips. What if the suspect doesn't show up? he thought. He wiped the perspiration from his forehead and altered his position in the car seat. Had he misjudged the intruder's intelligence? Suddenly he felt smothered in an electric blanket of the dark, hot July night.

Only the car's headlights selected the limited view that revealed their whereabouts. Finally, standing alone, a country-red building with a simple sign, Steve Zook's Woodcraft Shop. They pulled into the long lane that led back to the farmhouse. The car passed the woodshop and continued part way up the lane and stopped behind a corn crib where it would not be seen from the road.

"We can walk to the woodshop from here." said Detective Phillips.

The darkness that engulfed them was provided by the threat of a rain plus a typical Amish night - no electricity, no electric lights. They all turned on their flashlights and directed them toward the ground.

"Sammy, if you're right about this, it might help us solve some of the other three o'clock break-ins we've had over the last year," reported Detective Phillips.

"Sammy, tell us who this creep is," said Brian.

Sammy shook his head. "I can't prove it yet." He pointed his face toward the black sky and felt several raindrops. "We better hurry."

When they arrived at the woodshop, the rain was "makin' down" as the Amish might say. They took shelter at the side under the overhang. None of the three had thought to bring an umbrella even though the weather forecast called for rain. They hugged the building with their backs trying not to get wet.

"Sh, I hear something," whispered Sammy.

Detective Phillips peered around the corner through the rain. "Someone's walking up the driveway. I can see the beam of a flashlight."

The rain was falling faster now. The dark figure approached the shop. A large, black umbrella preceded the sinister-looking individual. It hurried to the overhang at the entrance to the woodshop. The umbrella collapsed, and the Amish man looked around as he put a key into the lock. It was Steve Zook!

"It's Steve Zook," whispered Brian. "Is he the one, Sammy?"

"No. He's here to let us into the shop and to give us some help if we need him. Hi, Steve, nasty night." Sammy's words fought through the rain and the three hustled in through the open door, following Steve.

"We want to thank you for your cooperation in our stakeout here tonight, or should I say early morning?" said Detective Phillips as they all tried to shake off the rain and dampness.

The Amish usually did not involve themselves with the police. They were inclined, because of their religion, to handle such matters themselves. But they were human, they were people, and they had feelings the same as anyone. And... Steve was young and modern.

"Oh, Sammy, Mrs. King wanted you to know that you-know-who stopped by earlier this evening and wanted to know if she had any tools to sell," reported Steve. "She done what you told her to say. That all her husband's tools were kept at the woodshop and had been sold to me."

"And then you had a visitor who was interested in buying your old tools and toolboxes. Right Steve?" continued Brian who appeared to be catching on to what Sammy meant by "shaking the bush."

Sammy smiled. "It's time to get ready for our indirectly invited guest."

Sammy and the detective had predetermined the suspect would probably enter through a rear window so as not to be detected by any passing horse and buggies and cars. Dark green shades covered all the windows in the shop. The far side of the woodshop, opposite the side containing the tool boxes, was selected to conceal themselves. A stack of precut oak wood provided an adequate hiding place. This vantage point afforded them a view of the rear windows and the bait: the wrench box.

"Is everybody awake? Keep your flashlights handy," whispered Sammy.

They all responded. Then quiet again. The darkness. The rain. The stillness. The musty smell of their damp clothes. The smell of wood reminding them of where they were. The far away sound of a passing car. The listening and hoping for something to happen soon. More darkness. More rain.

"Sammy, Sammy," came a faint voice from the darkness.

"Sh...what?"

It was Brian. "Sorry, I have to go to the bathroom. I can't hold it any longer."

Steve, as if by instinct, grabbed Brian's arm and led him around the unseen obstacles in the shop to the bathroom in the back corner. Some Amish businesses did have indoor plumbing.

"Please be quiet in there," said Sammy softly. "Don't turn the flashlight on and don't flush. If you hear any noise out here, stay in the bathroom. Don't come out."

They heard a bumping noise coming through the darkness.

"It's okay. I found it," said Brian in a strained whisper.

Muffled laughter started with the detective and spread to Steve. Sammy was not ready for humor. Not now. This is serious, he thought. Well, all right, no one could hear the smile on his face.

And the rain continued. And the darkness. And the tension. And there it was! The sound of footsteps outside the back center window. And Brian was still in the bathroom.

Sammy was aware that they all had heard it. He could feel it in the tension that was permeating the woodshop. Three unlit flashlights were pointed toward the window, waiting. It was three o'clock.

The metallic click was followed by a sliding sound. The window was open. In four seconds the flapping sound of the blind introduced a fifth occupant to the woodshop.

A lit flashlight traveled in the direction of the toolboxes. Within seconds the toolbox containing wrenches started to travel back toward the window. Sammy stepped back ready for action. An inhuman cry rang out. He had stepped on the cat's tail. The unexpected noise alerted the intruder. The toolbox was lowered to the floor. A single beam of light traveled to the pile of oak wood. Three beams shot back. The spillover was enough to illuminate the shop.

Caught in the light was a silhouette. The intruder was wearing dark clothes and a black ski mask. An obscure voice filtered through the cloth mask. "That you, Sammy? It is, isn't it?"

"Yes, it's me," answered Sammy.

The hooded figure headed for the open window. "Stand back or I'll slit you with this eight-inch blade."

"Drop the knife or I'll shoot you with this one-inch bullet," replied Detective Phillips.

Realizing that he couldn't make the window, the dark figure lunged at the bathroom door hoping for a way out.

"Brian, look out! He's coming in and he has a knife!" yelled Sammy as the three ran and pointed their flashlights toward the bathroom.

The small room echoed a resounding thud, groan, and a thump. Sammy feared the worse. He didn't want to lose his best friend, not in a stakeout that he had caused and carried out. He shouldn't have included Brian in this operation. It was too dangerous.

Sammy reached the door first and saw the body lying on the floor. It was still alive and groaning. Sammy gazed up and saw Brian standing on top of the toilet seat with a badly dented metal flashlight in his hand.

"Sorry, Sammy, I'll buy you another flashlight," said Brian, shrugging his shoulders.

"You okay? Hey, get out here," said Sammy

much relieved to find Brian unharmed. He grabbed Brian's arm as he stepped down from the toilet seat and pulled him out into the work area. This action allowed Detective Phillips to enter the bathroom, retrieve the knife from the floor, and drag the semi-conscious figure out into the light.

Steve had lit several propane-fed flames that added much needed light and a dramatic touch to the apprehension of the suspect.

Sammy and the detective lifted the resistant intruder to his feet. He struggled and tried to break loose, but they held firm.

"Brian, you may have the honor of taking the ski mask off so we can see who we have here," said the detective.

Brian, still fresh from his toilet seat caper and feeling tired and giddy, announced, "I have been waiting for this unveiling for a long time. Nothing will give me more pleasure than to..."

"Just do it, Brian. Just do it," said Sammy rolling his eyes and anxious to fit the last piece of the puzzle into place.

With a hard pull, the tight-fitting hood snapped off.

"It's Lloyd Smedley!" yelled Brian.

"Hello, Smedley. You solved the puzzle I see," added Sammy.

"Remember me?" asked the detective. "I talked to you about a year ago for selling stolen merchandise at the flea market. Now it seems we have proof."

"What? Wa... No, you have this all wrong. I wanted to drop off these pictures," said a very nervous Lloyd Smedley. He tried to compose himself as he reached inside his shirt pocket and displayed some photographs. "You know, Steve, for the glass case you're going to make for me."

"At three o'clock in the morning?" asked Detective Phillips.

"I was just passing by..."

"So you decided to break in," added Sammy, grabbing the photos. He was positive he would see one item in some of them. The quilt. "Look! you can understand why Smedley brought his camera into our shop the other day. He wanted to take pictures of the quilt. He pretended to take shots of the display case, which he did. But he made sure to include the quilt in the background. He needed the pictured squares to solve the puzzle."

"Why didn't he take the quilt with him the night of the break-in?" asked Brian.

"He would have, but I interfered. When he hit me and I fell, my arm got tangled in the quilt and pulled it from his hands."

"And when I crawled out the window," grumbled Smedley, "I dropped the dumb Bible. That's what got me in this mess - that Bible."

"You are what got you into this mess, Mr. Smedley," responded Sammy. "You should have read the other messages in the Bible."

Detective Phillips had the handcuffs on Smedley and read him his rights. "By the way, why did you do the break-ins at three o'clock in the morning?"

"If you go to bed early enough, it's a nice time to wake up and go to work," answered a flippant Lloyd Smedley.

Sammy turned and faced Brian. Neither of them were mentally or physically prepared to continue. Several questions had to be asked and answered before Sammy's logical mind could complete its program. But that would have to wait until morning. "Come on Brian, let's go home. You're sleeping over remember!"

"Right now I could sleep over anything," said Brian with his eyes closed and slumping in a standing position. "Do you think we'll remember any of this tomorrow morning?"

Chapter Nine

The Explanation

"Sammy, Brian, you awake?" Mrs. Wilson called through the bedroom door. "I know you haven't had much sleep, but a lot of people are down in the shop waiting to see you."

Sammy checked the alarm clock. It was already ten o'clock. Five hours sleep. That was almost enough, he thought.

"What's going on?" asked Brian half asleep.

"I guess by now everybody in Bird-in-Hand knows about Lloyd Smedley's arrest. Mom says the shop is full of people."

Brian was now wide awake. "Come on then. Our audience awaits."

Oh, brother, thought Sammy, wishing he could remain in bed and sleep.

Twenty minutes later Sammy and Brian was bombarded with compliments, congratulations, and handshakes. The crowd was a mixture of local regulars: Amish and non-Amish plus the bewildered tourists who were quickly filled in on the events of the last couple of days. Sammy did not feel comfortable in this situation. At first it was as if a large mass of humanity had engulfed him. As the novocain effect wore off, he became aware of individuals.

Steve Zook, who had been with Detective Phillips talking to some tourists, approached Sammy. "Thank you for what you done for me."

"Hey, it was you who helped us," replied Sammy.

"No, I mean the English people around here should know now I didn't have nothing to do with Amos' death, and I didn't take his money. Maybe now I'll get more business at the shop." Steve glanced at Brian. "And Brian, after you people left the shop, I went into the bathroom and..."

"Yes, what?" asked Brian.

"I flushed the toilet." Steve smiled and turned away. He was eager to retell the episode at his shop to the locals who were friendlier to him now as the facts were becoming known about Amos and his money.

Lynne Schlinkman, a young reporter from the local newspaper, had Mr. and Mrs. Wilson cornered behind a counter. Background information about Sammy would build readers' interest. Her article would cover not only the capture of Lloyd Smedley, but also the break-in and the mystery surrounding the Album quilt.

Mary, who previously had been interviewed by Lynne concerning the making of the quilt, was all smiles as she approached the two boys. Sammy watched as her untied cloth strings dangled from her white cap.

"I checked in with Mrs. King this morning. She's

very grateful to you boys. Imagine, Amos' money being in a dirty, old toolbox. I'm going to pick her up in the buggy Monday morning so the money will get safe in the bank."

"You be sure to take good care of her and the money," said Sammy.

Mary nodded, turned, and glanced again at the quilt her sewing group had produced. "Just think, we patterned it out from Amos' scratchin'. All that fuss over this silly quilt."

Sammy noticed Brian had walked over to a corner to receive attention from two friends from school. From Brian's motions, Sammy could tell he was enacting the downward plunge of the flashlight to Lloyd Smedley's head.

"Hey, Sammy," came a voice from a girl Sammy's age. Joyce Morris was also a member of the Brain Teasers Club at school. She was a pretty girl with brown hair and large hazel eyes. She wore a western style shirt tucked into her jeans. Of all the girls at school, if she was a boy, Joyce would be Sammy's second best friend. Girls usually intimidated Sammy, but Joyce, well, she was more like a sister.

"Congratulations, Sammy. You solved the big one didn't you, and without my help too," she kidded Sammy.

"Brian and I could have solved it sooner if you had helped," said Sammy knowing that it was true for Joyce had received many awards herself for problem solving.

Joyce examined the quilt and then said, "I have
a puzzle of my own to solve."

"What's that?" asked Sammy.

"How can I buy my younger sister a birthday gift
for three dollars when the birthday card alone costs two
dollars?"

"Is this the sister who collects baseball cards?"
asked Sammy.

"Yes, Linda. You should see her room, cards all
over."

"I know what I would do if I had a sister," said
Sammy. "I would create a birthday card just for her. On
her birthday I would hand it to her, put my arms around
her, and tell her I was glad she was my sister. And
then..." Sammy walked behind the baseball card counter,
slid open a door, and picked out a card. "And then I
would give her this Cal Ripken card which just happens
to cost three dollars today."

"Yuk," said Brian who had walked over during
the conversation. "Do you know what it's like having a
younger brother or sister? They can be a pain."

"Yeah, my sister can be a pain sometimes," said
Joyce, "an enjoyable pain though. I wouldn't ever want
anything to happen to her. Thanks, Sammy."

Sammy took the three dollars, put the card into
a paper bag, and handed it to Joyce. He looked again
at all the individuals who had come to offer congratulations.

"May I have your attention please," said Sammy timidly. "Brian and I want to thank you all for your kind words. I didn't do it alone. Brian Helm supplied specific ideas that helped solve this case." Sammy backed up two steps and put his arm around Brian's shoulder.

Brian blushed. "Sammy, don't forget. My birthday's next week."

"What made you suspect Lloyd Smedley in the first place?" asked the young news reporter.

"It was what he had said to me here at the shop the morning after the break-in. He mentioned the price of the Ken Griffy Jr. card as not being worth the three hundred dollars I was asking for it."

"I don't see anything wrong with that," replied Brian.

"I had placed the card with the price sticker of three hundred dollars in the case the night before the break-in. I changed my mind about selling the card and took it out of the case before the shop opened in the morning. The only way Smedley could have known about the three hundred dollar price was to have been in the shop that night."

Brian joined in, "And then I said something about seeing the backside of the moon. Right, Sammy?"

"Right, Brian." Sammy couldn't believe he had said that. But he was caught up in the flow. "When you lifted the moon poster to see its backside, I remembered what Mr. Smedley had said about the quilt. He said something about the whole back being ripped. How could he have known the entire back was torn? With the quilt hanging on the wall, you could only see the front and the rough edges."

"How did you know Lloyd Smedley would appear at Steve Zook's woodshop three o'clock in the morning?" inquired the reporter who was busy taking notes for the evening news.

"That was the easy part. I gave Mr. Smedley a shove in the right direction. After Brian and I solved the first picture in row three," Sammy pointed to the Album quilt hanging on the wall, "I visited Mr. Smedley at the flea market."

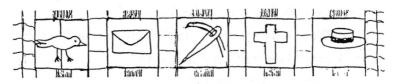

Brian maneuvered his way over to the quilt and pointed to the square. "It looks like the line is going through the bird, but it's really going through the square. The line divides the square in two. The bird becomes a wren and the word becomes wrench."

"At the flea market I casually discussed my 'theory' that maybe the first square of line three represented two letters. I figured," continued Sammy, "that Mr. Smedley would be able to come up with the word 'wrench' since he had already searched Mrs. King's deacon bench."

Sammy went on to explain how he then visited Mrs. King and Steve Zook, telling them he and Brian had solved the quilt puzzle. He instructed them on what to do and say should they have a visitor that evening.

"Mrs. King and Steve helped set up Mr. Smedley for the three o'clock break-in and his arrest," reported Detective Phillips.

Brian walked over to Sammy and whispered, "Somebody once said that everybody is famous for fifteen minutes in his lifetime."

"And?" said Sammy softly.

"According to my watch, you have two minutes left."

Sammy smiled, shook his head, and whispered, "Well, good, then I can go back to bed."

"What was the story on Officer Keener?" whispered Brian. "Did you ever find out?"

"Yeah," replied Sammy.

They both turned around and walked back toward the stairway so they would not be overheard. "I happened to mention it to Detective Phillips when we were making plans for last night. He said Officer Keener had a girlfriend living across the street. The night of the break-in he had gone into her house to see her. He should have been on duty in his patrol car. That's why he had a guilty look on his face when he saw me."

"Gee, and I thought he was the one."

"That is a good example why we should never accuse anyone without proof," stated Sammy.

Brian looked at Sammy for a while. "You know, Sammy, you're the best teacher I ever had."

Sammy waited for the punch line. There was none. Tears appeared in Sammy's eyes. This time logic could not control them.

Brian saw the tears and understood. "I know. You feel bad because you didn't get a reward for solving the puzzle."

"No, I don't expect anything," said Sammy as he wiped away the tears.

"Two-steppers don't take rewards. Right, Sammy?"

Sammy smiled. That was his reward.